The Daughter

The Daughter

Roberta Allen

Autonomedia

Portions of *The Daughter* first appeared
in the Penguin anthology *Between C & D*
and in the following magazines:
*Between C & D, Exquisite Corpse,
Mudfish, Five Fingers Review,
The Fiction Review, White Walls, Helicon Nine.*

The author wishes to thank
the Corporation of Yaddo and
the Virginia Center for the Creative Arts
for their hospitality.

Cover art and illustrations by the author.
Cover photograph by Elizabeth Schub.

Autonomedia
POB 568 Williamsburgh Station
Brooklyn, New York 11211-0568 USA
718-387-6471

We gratefully acknowledge publication assistance from the
New York State Council on the Arts.

Printed in the United States of America.

Contents

The Daughter

The Daughter

A group of girls and boys play by the pool; their cries and shouts and laughter echo under the high glass dome. The girl, who sits beside her father drinking lemonade, watches them wistfully. A plump girl, afraid she would be pushed, falls into the water. The boys laugh. The father and daughter laugh too, but now the girl is glad she is only a spectator. They sit beneath a striped umbrella. Sun glares through the skylit dome. Outside, melting snow, windblown, swirls through the sky. Potted palms line glass walls. The air feels tropical, steamy. The pool seems to be inside a giant greenhouse: to the daughter the pool seems as large as a lake. The girl is fourteen. Her father wants her to have fun, he says. He wants her to be easy and outgoing like him, but she is shy and nervous like her mother. 'Go over and introduce yourself!' Father urges the girl, but slumped in her seat, she shakes her head. At the hotel where they stay, the red velvet carpets, the sparkling chandeliers, the oval mirrors, the long cavernous corridors make the girl feel small and insignificant. The ceiling of their room is too high, the carved doors too massive, the windows too large. In the dining room the waiters remind her of morticians though she's never seen a funeral; the candle-lit room seems too dim, the draperies too dark, the silver plates too heavy. Even the marble tiles around the pool seem too smooth. The girl misses her cozy room at home where she dreams behind a closed door. Father thinks she dreams too much. Father has wrenched her from her world, whisked her away on this strange unwanted vacation. Despite her protests, Father pulls her from the chair, and pushes her toward the strange group of boys and girls. Shyly she approaches them as she feels her father's eyes upon her.

They are friendlier than she expected. She feels relieved. The boy with bright blue eyes smiles, takes her hand, and tosses her into the pool, then jumps in after her. He follows her underwater, then drags her down; they wrestle, she bobs up for air, and laughs. Chasing her, he pretends to be a crab, and tries to bite her feet. She thrashes madly through the water. Out of breath, laughing, she surrenders.

He grabs her feet, her waist, pulls her down below the surface. His long legs entwine her like a pair of snakes, his lips press against hers, his sinewy arms become a vice. She feels breathless, excited, her body tingles. Between strands of dripping hair she glimpses Father seated on the edge of his chair, his mouth open in surprise. The daughter ducks underwater, the blue-eyed boy beside her, his hands cup her breasts. Rising to the surface, she blushes, giggles. When she looks in Father's direction, she sees his wildly beckoning hand. She doesn't want to go: father was right; how much fun she was missing! Father stands up, scowling, impatient. 'I thought you wanted me to have fun!' the girl shouts angrily across the pool, surprised by the resonance of her voice. For a moment Father stares helplessly at the grinning boy with bright blue eyes, his arms around his daughter.

Woman in the Shadows

As the bus heads toward the ruins, the American woman stares out the window, and tries to forget her young Mexican lover who encouraged her to resume her travels. The bus speeds past flat fields with scattered ponds shaped like clouds. Tree roots like outstretched hands rise above peach-colored soil. Humpbacked cattle graze beneath flat-topped trees. The scenery brightens her mood. She turns toward the young man beside her, suddenly curious. The German student speaks fluent English, but answers her questions in a monotone voice. When she points out a tree filled with white birds against a dark sky, he doesn't share her enthusiasm. His long legs cramped, he sits stiffly, his handsome face mute. The woman, who once lived in Germany, talks about her past. Though the student is only three years younger than her lover, she feels old enough to be his mother. When they arrive at the ruins — the last passengers on the bus — the student runs off toward the pyramid after paying the ticket seller who seems to be alone at the site. To the woman, the half-cleared city surrounded by jungle, seems vast and forbidding. Fantastic masks decorate the pyramid. In thick stone walls doorways look as dark as the mouths of caves. Harsh shadows define two-headed serpents carved in stone. In the silence she hears the sound of creatures scampering through columned corridors. Shadows suggest lurking men and beasts. She gathers her courage and climbs a high platform, then enters one of several dark rooms in a row. From the doorway she spots the German wearing a baseball cap turned backwards, sitting high on the terrace of a temple. As she walks toward him down the narrow dirt road in the midday heat she breathes easier though he doesn't seem to notice her. Halfway up the steps of the temple she pauses, afraid to climb higher as the student descends lost in thought, and takes a narrow path through a dense thicket. The woman follows at a distance, but in the darkness of the forest, decides to turn back. When she returns to the entrance, the German is already there. The ticket seller says the last bus left, but another bus will stop at a nearby village. Together on the empty road waiting to flag down a passing car, the student and the woman laugh at their poor timing. But after the ride as they wait in the village, they sip their sodas in silence. On the old bus the woman loses sight of the student amidst the crowd of ragged Indians carrying baskets and bundles, children and baby chicks. At the station the woman looks for the German, for without him the cobbled streets, the shops, the markets of this town feel as strange as the ruins.

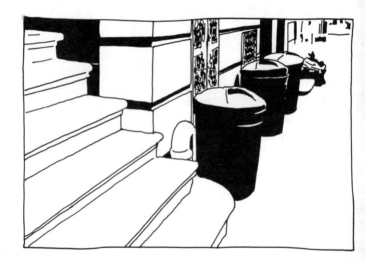

Family Life

My friend's parents own a typewriter shop. When a customer hears their accents and assumes they are German, they quickly correct the mistake. The Austrian couple share little beside the typewriter shop, two children, and their loathing of Germans. My friend's mother is obese. She regards her daughter and me with disdain when she's aware of us at all. Her mother's lover for twenty-odd years — also Austrian — helps her mother keep the books for the business. I often see him sitting beside her mother at the desk, pondering figures in the dark cramped living room. I've never really seen his face. He keeps his head lowered beneath a wide-brimmed fedora he never removes in my presence. Everyone mistakes him for her husband at first. My friend's father spends his time with whores when he's not in the shop. When at home, he flirts with me and all his dauqhter's friends. He invites me to movies, shows and concerts, but

I know what's on his mind. My friend sends him away with a flick of her wrist, as if he was an unwanted child, but he returns undaunted each time. Her mother's sour expression, turned in his direction, becomes a sneer. Her brother, on his rare visits home from the army, also treats him with scorn. Her father doesn't seem to mind, in fact, he seems to welcome the abuse he inspires.

My mother is shocked when I relate the details of their family life. I wonder why mother acts so shocked. Did she forget my father was a gambler hunted by the mob before he took his own life? Or does she still believe things like that only happen in movies.

The Hotel

Some would say this is just a hotel by the road but I know better. The billboard with a thatched roof faces the highway. From the other side the thick white-washed wall looks like an altar with two deep niches holding small earthenware pots. Nearby, clusters of fuschia blossoms glow like stars in small green skies. Trees with fronds too thick to tear rise tangled, and cut a zig-zag patch of dazzling blue above. A woman with joyous outstretched arms is only a branch on a tree. Drooping fronds hide nesting fruits, yellow-green and heavy. A web of roots binds the shards of a clay urn. The violet sky dims, and the jumble of vines like thick rubber bands, fade-out. White lawn chairs, their delicate legs poised on a platform of paved stone round the pool, engage in casual conversation with the moon, the stars. A truck roars past. A bus simulates thunder. The spotlight illuminates a praying mantis on the arm of a chair, looking like a leaf. In the dark, army ants, blindly marching, blacken my feet in their path. They feel like lit matches on my skin. Some crawl up my legs and send me screaming. I jump in the pool to rid myself of ants while the house boy sprays pesticide: for a moment I forget the magic; forget my lover who owns the hotel.

Africa

*H*ere in deep jungle I poke with a stick behind bricks, banana peels, broken bottles, beer cans, and charred wood beams. I dig beneath old tires, plastic bags, and mattress springs, searching for pink stones more precious than any precious jewel. I keep them hidden from my mother in my school bag. Weeds grow so high I can't see the red brick block where I live: all the buildings look the same.

In damp earth I plant carved wood stems, once table legs I suspect. Between white puffs of milkweed, twisted metal pipes turned orange and green, look like slithering snakes. Tangled black wires grow like vines without leaves. Between concrete chunks from fallen castles, bits of colored glass gleam. From royal gowns, flower-printed scraps of cloth, lie faded beside dandelions. Weeds grow everywhere. Even on the blob of burnt foam rubber something green is growing. With my stick I stir a murky pool; iridescent violet, blue, and golden swirls shimmer in sunlight. Behind a burnt-out car, I find a shoe, the remains of a traveler. I stumble, and fall in a patch of dead leaves. If I cry out no one will hear though sometimes I talk to the natives. While digging for worms I listen for bird calls and watch for signs of wild beasts; the black tomcat who hisses, the tabby who hides, the stray mongrel who sniffs the air and yelps. I brush a swarm of gnats from my face while mosquitoes and horse flies buzz around my head. The dead mouse I found yesterday has disappeared.

When I come home Mother slaps my hands. 'You're filthy!' she shrieks, and shoves me in the bath. 'God knows what you touched!' she cries out. Her face reminds me of the gray stone gargoyles that scared me once. Mother forbids me to go to Africa again. She doesn't know about Asia. Or Polynesia. But I know that bulldozers are several blocks away. Eurasia has fallen and Gondwana has sunk. My travels after school take me further and further from home. Soon the world will be filled with red brick blocks, and all my continents will be lost like Atlantis.

Return

When she first arrived in this small provincial town, she was certain she had found the place where she belonged, far from the grayness of her home. On her second trip, inching through the crowd, she tries to capture the excitement she felt before when passing through these hot narrow dusty streets. But the broad brown faces she found so innocent and open, now appear cunning, suspicious, spiteful. When she looks closely at the native dress that charmed her months ago, she sees grime encrusted in the cloth. She watches beggars crouch in doorways. She sees packs of ragged boys roam the streets. Where are the laughing children? The colorful weavings? The fired pots? Stalls filled with plastic pails and aluminum pans surprise her. She sees the face of an old wizened woman repeated on the turkeys in the old woman's stall. She stares at baby chicks and crows crammed into wire cages. She watches a squirrel madly somersault in his tiny metal cell. The vendor selling sweet breads cheats the woman. On the plaza thick black smoke oozing from the bus engulfs her. Away from noise and fumes, she watches a tiny broken figure in a battered wheelchair being pushed by a barefoot boy down a cobbled street. Even the gray clouds look menacing to her. Where is the clear cerulean sky? In vain she tries to recall the town as she saw it the first time. Was everything she saw then an illusion? Is she the same woman who was here before?

Daydream

My half-sister is shrieking in the front seat of the car while her husband — a gambler like our father — races through the mountains at top speed. This trip feels like a roller coaster ride. My half-sister's husband can't wait to reach Las Vegas and lose his wife's money. Their son and daughter hold each other tight in the back seat where I sit too. My half-sister's daughter — who is older than me! — is also shrieking. I keep my nose pressed against the window glass. I am not afraid.

My half-sister's husband laughs gleefully as he makes a hairpin turn on the steep mountain road without slowing down or honking the horn first. As we round each bend, my half-sister lets out a scream and begs him to slow down. The more she pleads, the wilder he drives. 'You'll kill us all!' she cries. But her husband is having too much fun to listen. I don't listen either. I don't let anyone disturb my daydream: I am home in New York with this French boy named Jean. We are rowing on the lake in Central Park. We are having a very good time.

The Forest

In the dining room where we have just finished dinner, small flames dance in glass globes under a thatched roof. Outside, thick woods surround us. Through the window dimly outlined silhouettes of palm trees, banana plants, gently sway under magnified stars. The pool shimmers. Like a bright pebble a shooting star sails across the night. The iguana's tail is visible for an instant. Bats, in uncertain orbits, dart back and forth over the pool. In the stillness I can hear the earth breathe. In my lover's arms — I smell his sweet hair, each strand feels fragile — I lie in wonder lazily following the slow motion of the ceiling fan. Each morning I watch while swiftly moving hands cut-down, tear-out, rip apart the encroaching greenness that threatens to overwhelm us; to knot us in its inextricable embrace. Inside I feel the forest take root. I am a detour in its path. I understand its persistence. There is a forest, a deep wood inside myself and my lover; our roots are interwoven, our leaves mesh. Like something green and growing I reach out and kiss my lover's hair.

Bananas

On the top floor of the tenement next door, they keep green bananas with black splotches on the windowsill. I watch the bananas blacken and grow soft in the sunlight. Grandma says the bananas are rotten. Grandma says, 'You mustn't watch those people! They disgrace our neighborhood.' Our building has a doorman and a marble lobby.

At night I have the best view when I peek through my pink lace curtains. By then Grandma has gone home so I can be alone in my room while Father snores in a chair in the living room and Mother silently fumes in the kitchen.

My neighbors keep their windows wide open in summer. I can see their bathroom with stained green walls. Sometimes three or four little girls and boys splash in the tub together beneath a bare bulb. The grown-ups scream

29

and shout, but laugh too. They play loud Latin music on the radio. Sometimes I glimpse a face as a dark hand grabs a banana. The women have red or fuschia fingernails and bright lips. A few times I saw an old wizened woman with frizzy white hair. Her hand had purple veins that stuck out. I could see she had no teeth when she talked. Must be a grandma, I thought.

My grandma often imitates their Spanish; she makes a face, wrinkles her nose, and rolls her tongue around real fast; she makes sounds that make no sense. Grandma says they smell bad. The country they come from is dirty and poor, she says. All they do is make babies and lie in the sun on the beach. Someday I'd like to see that country.

Departure

Seated in the near empty dining room of the hotel near the ruins in Yucatan, the Canadian, middle-aged, complains about his digestion, thinks he suffers from amoebas. At home in Vancouver, he tells the American woman, they know nothing about tropical diseases. His wife, a bit tipsy, agrees. The young and handsome hotel owner, with pale green eyes, sits opposite his lover, the American woman. When the hotel is slow, he has time to join his guests. He seems comfortable in his open shirt although the weather is unusually cold.

In Vancouver the wife is a pilot. Brave or foolhardy, she enjoys flying her small plane in bad weather over lonely stretches of land and sea. Her husband builds sail boats for the rich. With his sunken cheeks, wide mouth, and large prominent teeth, he reminds the American of Mayan skulls carved in stone at the ruins.

31

Meeting these people at home wouldn't feel so special, the American thinks to herself. At home, she wouldn't feel so open, so genuinely interested in someone other than herself. But here, the air feels charged, electric. She can see the Canadians feel the sparks too.

At times, the Mexican loses the drift of the conversation in English, but the others patiently repeat or explain what he missed. The wife grows excited describing the blackberry to the Mexican. Her passion for blackberries equals the American's passion for her young Mexican lover. The wife draws the vine on a napkin, describes the color, the taste, its use in pies and compotes. But when they translate the name into Spanish, with a dictionary the wife staggered off to find, for a moment, the Mexican looks disappointed.

The Canadian man talks about drugs planted on boats in the Caribbean. He says, 'The Coast Guard confiscates the boats they raid. The owners never see them again!'

'Must be good for your business!' says the American, laughing.

When they discuss their travels, the American, wishing to hide her age from her young Mexican lover, lies about the dates of her trips.

The Mexican wouldn't want to live in Spain, he says, though his family comes from Barcelona. Even the States — where he studied — don't tempt him. 'I am happy here,' he says.

When the clock strikes twelve, all four show surprise. The Canadian couple seem sorry the evening is over. The wife says, 'We've had a wonderful time!' Even the Mexican, who tries to hide his feelings, looks pleased.

Only the American looks sad. She smiles wistfully at the Mexican who feels embarassed in front of the couple. She smiles wistfully as she thinks about her departure. She wishes every night could be like this. But next week she will be home; next week her lover will have different guests; next week nothing will be the same, nothing but the Mayan skulls carved in stone.

Summer

Several campers have succumbed to mysterious maladies and gone home, the girl's best friend among them. The girl has qualms about staying at the summer camp, but the camp director tells her: 'If you give up now, you will give up all your life!' Fortunately her new friend is not afflicted with anything mysterious though last week she suffered whiplash when the truck stopped short. Now she wears a surgical collar. Even the collar becomes her, the girl muses. The girl wishes she looked like her friend. She looks at photomat pictures they took together the day they hitched a ride and sneaked to town. Beside her friend's sculpted cheekbones and delicate features, her chubby face and wispy hair makes her sigh.

When she isn't dreaming about her friend, she dreams about the swimming counsellor who thinks of nothing but his looks. She imagines words he would say to her if he turned his mind away from his muscles. Like her friend he has green eyes, but his green eyes look painted on his copper skin.

Each morning the girl waits outside the mess hall for the tall thin figure of her friend who comes to breakfast sleepy-eyed, wearing her steady's soiled shirt. The girl worries that her friend might leave with her steady, or, like a wild flower, she might die before the summer's end. Then only the swimming counsellor would remain; only this boy with his biceps flexed, this boy who doesn't see her.

The Pool

In town, behind the crumbling villa, now a hotel, a profusion of palms and tropical plants line the pool. In the water, reflections of the trees quiver, and clouds glide over the surface. A lizard floats, helpless. Hornets and dragon flies loop through the air, their wings sputter.

By the pool, the woman waits for a man who was her lover several months ago. Late last night she arrived, unexpected, at his hotel. The house boy opened the door. She didn't look familiar to the house boy, who has greeted many guests. At the desk, she signed her name.

The sky darkens as the woman waits by the pool. The water becomes murky; trees and clouds blend together in a deep turquoise hue tinged with brown. The woman sighs. A breeze ripples the surface. Sounds from the street behind the thick whitewashed wall seem miles away.

She wonders if her lover has gone to his other hotel near the ruins. Perhaps she won't see him at all. But still she listens to footsteps. She waits for his footsteps to find her.

The sky clears as her feet dangle in the pool. Shimmering water is reflected in dancing patterns of light on the wall until a sudden cloud hides the sun. The patterns on the wall grow dim. The lizard, lifeless now, drifts in the darkest corner of the pool. Footsteps cease.

Late at night he enters her room. His breath reeks of beer. His ruffled shirt is wide open. The damp stucco walls sweat, ooze with moisture. They perspire despite the ceiling fan. Fumes of pesticide taint the room. But she smells only his hair. Only the fragrance of his hair reminds her of the nights they spent together. She moves her hands along his smooth skin, trying to remember. Near dawn he returns to his room. The woman goes out to the pool. She eases herself into still dark water, still trying to remember.

The Lie

The little girl steps in her father's footprints in the sand of the poor man's beach. Father says she mustn't tell Mother he brought her here. After all, they are not poor, though Father was poor when he came here as a boy. The receding tide leaves a million oyster shells strewn on shore. Father and the girl climb rocks along the jetty, rocks clothed in sleek black satin, and green velvet moss. The girl finds snails small as a pea. From a darkskinned woman in a booth on the boardwalk, Father rented her a swim suit. In a damp dark locker room Father helped her slip it on. From a fold in the cloth a cockroach escaped. The girl started. Father laughed. The girl remembered Mother's words to Father: 'Don't you dare take her to that foul beach!' Father and the girl lie in the sun between families who speak foreign tongues. To the girl, Father doesn't seem like a grown-up anymore. Like two children they prod a dying jellyfish with twigs, with sticks they maul the sand till they reach water. On the way home Father buys her a piece of forbidden fudge. Perhaps it is wrong for the little girl to feel this close to Father. Perhaps it is wrong of Father to behave like a child. Perhaps this is why when Father fibs, she nervously giggles, and Mother sees through his lie.

Menage

On a large moonlit lake in the Guatemalan jungle, a stocky German banker from Rio discretely fondles the breasts of two American girls lying languidly in the bottom of an old boat. He smiles to himself; he can hardly believe his good luck. On a whim he followed the girls when his conference was cancelled though they only met once in Guatemala City. He raises a bottle of wine to his lips, then passes it round to the girls. The small girl, her green eyes closed, imagines herself alone with the banker while her friend, tall and dark-eyed, devises schemes to win the banker for herself. The girls know about his wife and children, but they don't mind; this is their vacation. The lake gently ripples as the boat glides slowly through the water. Droning insects muffle the sound of the outboard motor. The boatman pretends to see nothing but the lake.

At dusk, the trio swam off the dock of a tiny island. Half-hidden by a raft, the small girl and the banker made love. The tall girl ducked underwater so she wouldn't see,

41

but the water amplified their cries and moans. Upset, she swam to shore and waited, staring with tearful glassy eyes at the purplish shadows of the overhanging palms in the lake. By the time her companions returned, her eyes were dry, and a forced smile appeared upon her lips. As the German led them to the waiting boat, he embraced both girls, giving hope to the tall one.

The wine finished, the banker orders the boatman to head for shore. Few lights shine in the scattered villages on the lake. In a little hotel by the water, the banker rents a room for three.

Lush flowers fill the courtyard. In the tiny room, three narrow cots line the walls. They undress, and he turns out the lights. Softly, the banker creeps into bed with the tall girl while the small girl pretends to sleep, but she hears their panting, their moaning, the creaking springs. The small girl clenches her fists, and bites her lips while tears glisten in her eyes. After their final throes of passion, she hears the German return to his bed; she listens to his loud snores. All night she lays awake. In the morning, she can barely control her fury. She rises, shaking with rage; she glares at the banker and the tall girl, still in their beds. The German knows a terrible scene is about to take place: he can almost hear her screams and shouts, the crashing chair, the slamming door in the terrible silence. Lying on his back, he closes his eyes and wishes he could wake-up in Rio. Only the boatman, peeking through the window slats, wishes he could take his place.

On the Beach

Father laughs as Mother hides a network of thin blue veins on her thigh with make-up. Mother doesn't like the beach. She doesn't swim. Her skin is fair. She burns easily. Father laughs derisively at the scarf tied over her sun hat. With her sunglasses on, she doesn't look like my mother. Father paces back and forth. Suddenly he dives into the waves, disappears, until his head bobs up beyond the breakers. He swims far out to sea, so far out the life guard blows his whistle, waves him back. Mother frowns when she glances from her book. 'He's just showing off,' she says. Returning to the beach blanket Father laughs, dripping wet his muscles glisten. Mother pays no attention when he sprays her. 'Come on, you need some exercise,' Father laughs, dragging Mother from her hide-out under the umbrella. Mother struggles, squirming, twisting, kicking. He pulls her to the water's edge. 'That's enough!' she cries. 'You're no fun,' Father says, and turns away. Lifting me high in the air, he carries me on his shoulders into the surf. I scream, 'Don't drop me!' He lowers me gently into the water, and with my arms around his neck, I kick and splash in the waves. When we return, mother is wrapped like a cocoon in her white beach robe under the umbrella. She reads her book, pretends we aren't there. Father and I build a castle in the sand. We pretend we don't care when mother ignores us.

The Reluctant Traveler

In the rainforest, a woman wearing a yellow poncho stands under the eaves of the ruined palace, and nervously follows the paths of circling hornets high above her head while waiting for the rain to let up. Stone steps glisten, and puddles form. She grows anxious at the thought of descending the steep and slippery stairs. Trees and vines, dangling from the roof, tremble. Chilled, she huddles against the cold stone wall. She wonders what ancient rites were performed in the gloomy chambers. Dark clouds hide dense jungle. The sound of rain muffles the strange cries of birds. The ruins are almost deserted. But a few solitary tourists like herself find shelter in the temples. The woman thinks about her journey, shudders as she recalls the fourteen hour bus trip through the mountains as she lay ill. She thinks about her lover who waits patiently at home for her return. Even her boss had wished her well before she left. She wonders what foolish whim has led her to this place. She remembers her father's words when she was a child: 'That girl is too brave!' he said. She wonders what he would say now if he was still alive, if he could see her standing here alone in the rainforest. She wonders why she still needs to impress her father.

The Dog

I am in the hall alone. Where has Father gone? The dog is big, the hall is dark and long and winding; there are many doors on either side. Behind which door do I belong? The dog barks; he is black and queer-shaped, with clumps of curly fur protruding from his skin. Which door hides Mother and Grandma? The dog comes closer. I see the dog's bared teeth and gleaming purple gums, his long thick wet tongue; he pants. The stairs. I see the stairs. I look down, I am dizzy; ten flights of curving steps — to where? Why are the banisters so high, the marble stairs so wide and steep and smooth? The dog growls, watching me with fiery eyes as I stand against the wall. I bang on the closest door, shouting. A woman wearing a bandana opens the door. Her mouth is painted red high above her lipline. I watch her call the dog, then drag it inside. With her hand on my shoulder, she leads me down the hall. Mother and Grandma look at me surprised: they didn't know I was gone. How could they notice, it's so dark in there since Father left.

At the Crossroads

The woman rents a room at the only hotel within walking distance of the ruins. At dawn she will flag down a passing bus. The latch on the door of her room is loose. The toilet — without a seat — doesn't flush. Outside, screeching trucks halt abruptly, and two thin horses stand motionless in caked mud. She enters the restaurant with a low thatched roof where a group of travelers, loud and drunk, stagger round and sing off key. The woman eats her dinner quickly at a table in the corner, and returns to her room with a sigh of relief. The thought of the ruins restores her spirits.

The sight of the small silent city exposed to the sun filled her with sympathy. She felt at home here. The curve and tilt of a wall against the sky was not foreign but familiar, endearing. She felt the delicate figures on the faded mural were painted only for her eyes. A slice of beach at the foot of the cliff seemed destined to be her discovery. She wandered through tombs and temples and palaces and watchtowers with tiny rooms and dim corridors smelling of mildew. She scrambled up and down broken stairs, over terraces, through crumbling archways, past heaps of fallen stone. Like a child in a vast playground she climbed and crawled and peered through every crevice. She played games she never knew as a child. In a cavern beneath a palace she crouched by murky water seeking the reflection of the child she had become. At night in the dark in the room by the cross-roads she dreams of a little girl in a tiny chamber, fast asleep, all alone.

The Little Doll

Two old women, one with a child beside her, sit in the sun on folding chairs in front of the bank. The old woman with crimson lips looks at the silent child holding her grandmother's hand. 'She's such a little doll!' the woman says. Proudly Grandmother smiles and sits more erect in her chair. She smoothes the child's dress, making sure there's not a crease. Wearing a clean starched pinafore and patent leather shoes, the child comes here daily with her grandmother. While they admire her she stands so still she barely seems to breathe. Even when the women's talk turns to gossip, she continues to stand there, motionless. Grandmother never lets the child get dirty; never takes her to the park. 'She's so well-behaved!' the old woman says when she sees the child still hasn't moved. The child never thinks about running away; she knows Grandmother won't let her out of sight. But Grandmother can't see the make-believe world where the little girl plays while her dreamy eyes gaze into the distance.

The Blanket

During siesta in the hotel room of a small town near Monte Alban, the woman admires the handwoven Indian blanket she bought at the market. She gazes at the blanket draped over a chair as she lies on the bed. She admires the muted tones, the geometric patterns, but she thinks about the blanket she has at home, one not so beautiful nor finely made that she purchased at a market years ago. The woman who was very poor in her youth, and rarely bought herself a present, remembers her joy when she bought that blanket. On her travels she no longer counts pennies, no longer chooses the cheapest lodgings. Out of curiosity she asks to see a room in a dingy hotel. Although vivid flowers brighten the courtyard, weeds sprout between broken tiles, and rotting fruits hang from stunted trees. The bare room with a cracked concrete floor is damp and dark, a tiny skylight the only window. A bureau, old and worn, stands against a green discolored wall. Black specs freckle the mirror. A frayed bedspread with suspicious stains covers the lumpy bed. She hears young boys laughing in the street. She imagines herself asleep in this room, but the woman she sees is still a young girl.

The Hat Pin

The hat pin I carry in my bag doesn't make me feel safe. But it makes Mother feel better. Mother gave me the hat pin to defend myself. Mother gave me the hat pin in case they try to get me at school.

Father is dead. He killed himself last week. They think Father left us a lot of money. When they call, they think Mother is lying when she laughs and says, 'He left us nothing!' She laughs even though they threaten my life. I am not laughing.

Every day I take a cab to school and carry a hat pin in my bag. In the halls I look behind me when I walk. On the stairs I listen for strange footsteps. The police say they can't do anything. They can't do anything at all even though the men have threatened my life. They can't do anything until the men do something to me!

I first saw them at the funeral. They wore fedoras which covered their eyes. They had bulges under their jackets which Mother said were guns. 'They are checking us out,' Mother said. 'They've come to see what we look like.'

Father told me he would do it. Father told me that last morning in the cab. Father was going to his store. I was going to school. I said nothing when Father told me. I said nothing even though I knew what he would do. 'I owe them so much money!' he said.

I said nothing because I was afraid that I would cry. I didn't want him to see me cry. I didn't want him to see that I would miss him.

He always told me to be strong. So I was acting strong. I was acting as though I'd be all right without him. Now I am sorry I acted so strong. If I had cried I might still have a father. If I had told him not to do it I might not need a hat pin in my bag.

Father is gone, but the gray cloud surrounding him for three weeks is still here. For three weeks Father took pills and slept. For three weeks Father was living his death. Now he's left his death for us to live.

The Crisis

In a small Latin American town, in midsummer, a tall Dutch girl paces back and forth in front of the cafe where the few tourists gather who stop overnight en route to other destinations. The Dutch girl, thin and nervous, her front tooth badly chipped, casts sidelong glances at the customers, searching for an appropriate stranger. At last, at a table alone she spies a woman, middle-aged, deeply tanned, her clothes well-worn and dusty. Without hesitation she approaches her. 'May I talk to you?' she says in English, her eyes intense, her voice conveying urgency. The woman, who feels lonely, bored, and languid from the heat, pulls out a chair. Sitting down, the Dutch girl confides, 'I have a problem. I am three months pregnant. I must know — is it too late to have an abortion?'

The woman is silent for several seconds as she recalls her abortion twenty years ago. She says, 'You must have it done right away.'

'I am leaving the man I live with here,' the girl continues. 'Where do you live?' she asks the woman.

'New York,' the woman replies, uneasily.

'Is it easy in New York to have an abortion?' the girl asks, nervously rubbing her arms.

'Easy, yes, but I don't know if it's cheap,' the woman says, sizing up the girl's old jeans and T-shirt. The woman wonders if she will ask for money.

'I heard there is a cheap flight from Miami to London. Perhaps I should go there,' the Dutch girl says, uncertainly.

'How have you and your friend managed to live here?' the woman asks, distracted as ragged Indian children aggressively peddle their wares.

'My friend is from Brazil. He's a mime. We have an act. We play for people on the street. We travel from town to town. It's a good living. He wants to keep the child.'

'Are you sure you want to leave him?' the woman asks.

'I don't want to be tied down. I want to grow. Someday I'll get married. I'll raise children, but not now.'

The woman listens as the girl who left Holland two years before, recounts her adventures on a fishing boat in Alaska, and as a waitress in Costa Rica before she came here. She envies the girl's courage though she also travels alone, but only for a few weeks. Her tales remind the woman of the travels of her youth. She understands the girl's terror of her pregnancy, her fear of the future, her need to find her way. The woman, who blames herself for having lost her sense of adventure, feels suddenly glad she has lost her youth.

Longing

Wine

She awaits his arrival in mid-afternoon with the same anticipation she felt as a child. At the sound of the bell downstairs, the girl runs to the mirror and smoothes her hair though not a strand is out of place. Carrying a bottle of wine, the middle-aged man eagerly climbs the stairs to her apartment. His intentions are transparent to the girl who stands by her open door watching his accent: she knows the bottle of wine is not for her but for the man who needs courage.

She pours him a drink while he stands a few feet away, his courage fleeing faster than wine from the bottle. His fondness for the girl frightens him. As he shifts weight from one foot to another, he feels the floor become a sea. Suddenly, a barrage of bitter words about his wife escapes his lips. The girl quietly listens. Her sympathy and patience comfort him once more as he lets loose his rage. He feels the floor solidify beneath his feet while he stares at the parket pattern. Grateful, he hugs the girl. On the couch they kiss, grope, embrace like adolescents. Once more afloat on a sea, the man pulls away. The girl raises the glass of wine to his lips, but already it is too late.

Specter

On screen in the cinema, a married man makes love to his mistress. The girl watching, shakes her head, amused by his choice of film. Discretely she glances at the man beside her, barely breathing, who sits poised like a passenger on a plane awaiting take-off, each hand tightly cupped around the arm rest. His thoughts are miles away, she observes, her mood darkening. His presence here is nothing more than a specter, she concedes. He can't even enjoy his voyeurism. She removes her elbow from the arm rest between them. Sulking, she swings over to the far side of her seat, trying to attract his attention and deny his existence at the same time. The image of his wife — whom she's never seen — looms larger in her mind than the frantic figures on screen who pale in the fiery light of her rage.

Figures

Outside the restaurant he asks for a quarter for the parking meter. A quarter! She can't believe her ears. While the girl searches through her purse, he mentally subtracts her tip from the dinner he just paid. When they buy beer at the corner store, he pays her share — though he calculates his loss. Upstairs, they sit together on her sofa, drinking beer. Continuing to fret about his money, he figures out the cost of his divorce. The girl listening, betrays her impatience by moving closer to him. Resisting his impulse, he leans forward, concentrating with difficulty on his computations until he regains control. In an unguarded moment he slips his arm around her waist. As though suddenly aware of her presence, he asks her weight. The calculator starts working in her head. Is he figuring pound for pound, she wonders, how much it will cost to keep me?

Game

Watching the ball game, the couple cheer when their team scores a run, hugging with excitement. Here in the ball park where emotions are pinned to fly balls, base hits, and home runs, they find release. Amidst the roar of the crowd, their fears and desires pass unnoticed. During a break, the man and the girl, holding hands, descend the stadium stairs and head toward the food stalls. Joyfully she eats junk food she otherwise hates. With childlike enthusiasm she bites off a bit of sausage; the juice drips down her chin too fast for her napkin. They sip the same beer, sweating in summer sun. With a handkerchief the man dabs his neck and forehead. Together they lick a chocolate ice cream cone which leaves traces on his chin, her nose; they laugh. The girl looks up at the sky, dazzled that they share the same earth.

Trip

Tonight the man leaves on a trip abroad. Terrified of being alone, he holds her tight. Assuring him over and over that his trip will go well, the girl begins to feel like his mother. The present blurs before his eyes. When he tries to focus on the future he sees a map without markers, an ocean with everlasting waves that find no shore. Helpless, he clings to the girl, his only anchor. Awakened to desire, he recoils like a child with a delayed reaction touching fire. The peak of his crisis past, he sighs, then drifts back in her arms, but with one eye open like a small boat suspended by a rope in a rippling sea.

Divorce

One day the man telephones the girl to announce his divorce has just become final. 'Let's have lunch to celebrate,' he says. Arriving early at the restaurant, the girl sighs. All these months of waiting are finally over. At the table where he joins her, sun streams through the window. 'You look ten years younger,' she tells him. Laughing, he unfolds plans of his newly purchased house, pointing out the high arched windows in the master bedroom, and the screened-in porch facing the yard: 'where we will breakfast,' he says. When she suggests they return to her place, however, his eyes darken.

'No, I must pack,' he replies, his mind suddenly distracted by details of his move.

'Surely you could wait an hour longer after all these years,' she implores.

But his mind is made-up; he will return to the house he still shares with his wife, where he sleeps on the sofa downstairs. As he drops her off in the car by her door, he says with relief, 'At last I am free.'

She wonders: When will he stop resisting me?

Dream

The man sits wide-eyed on the couch in the girl's apartment, gazing uncertainly at the fireplace; the knick-knacks he admired on the mantelpiece look different since his divorce. He cannot face the girl cooking dinner in the alcove yet, for she too, seems changed. Searching for a reference point, he finds only tilted walls and doors that don't fit. The girl conceals her excitement over his unexpected visit while he paces the floor, impatient for the future now; that he may see and know everything; no more surprises. So long as he keeps moving, her unspoken words can't make him stay; he can leave any time. Rest, he wants rest, but he keeps pacing, afraid he will root like a plant if he's still.

He collapses helpless on the couch after dinner, yielding to the fingers that stroke his hair. Eyes closed, breathing deeply, he allows her fingers to knead his shoulders, his neck.

Past midnight the two figures lie tangled among rumpled bed clothes. His head sunk back against the pillow, he stares at the ceiling. 'I'm not ready for this,' he whispers. Imagining their future life together, the girl scarcely hears his words. He rises, quickly dressing. At the door, her soothing voice magnifies his guilt. The girl, however, perceives his departure as only a detail in her dream.

River

On impulse, the girl takes a vacation in the country while the man stays with friends out of town — friends he promised to visit with her. Even his week-long escapes don't defeat her. She tells herself: 'My patience will outlive his fear.'

Standing on the river bank, the girl hesitates before her swim; the river looks calm though signs warn of rapids. Her slow and easy crawl leads her downstream toward a group of boys splashing off a rocky island in the center of the river. Suddenly she finds herself sucked in a swiftly moving current; panic grips her as she glimpses white water ahead. The boys, a few feet away, play, unaware of her presence. Using all her strength, her hands catch hold on a jagged boulder; the craggy surface scratching her flesh as she hoists herself out of the water.

As she rests on the river bank, her thoughts turn to him. Trying to forget her fears, she dives once more despite the warnings.

Yard

Beneath tall oak trees with gnarled trunks, the man and the girl eat their dinner. The last flickering rays of sunlight barely illuminate the backyard overgrown with weeds. In the clearing, a weathered bench serves as their improvised table. They sit on worn wicker chairs with uncertain legs. A gentle breeze stirs. Faint strains of music drift in the evening air; that sound, the only sign of human life beyond the high white fence enclosing them.

The man moved into his house the day before. The girl is his first visitor. Unpacked cartons crowd the floors. Earlier, he led the girl through unfurnished rooms covered with faded wallpaper. A stray chair, a table, abandoned by the previous owners, stand like unwanted guests. The girl admired the wood paneling as she followed him up the stairs. She pictured the two of them removing wallpaper, painting walls, arranging furniture.

In the yard where they eat Chinese food on paper plates, the girl, who lives only an hour away in the city, imagines herself in a foreign land filled with luxuriant greenery; the neglected garden colored by hope; a friendly jungle where life is simple, deadlines don't exist. The breeze has extinguished the candle. Their voices fleetingly etch the darkness. The man, nervously toying with his fork, suggests they go inside. When he turns on the kitchen light, a black furry caterpillar crawls among grains of rice. The girl laughs; just another sign of life's abundance spilling over. Simple things. She can't see the terror in his eyes.

Party

At his mid-afternoon party the girl knows his every step though they barely speak and unfamiliar faces block her view. Playing host in high spirits, he moves with ease from guest to guest, his manner warm and lively, his eyes flashing. He laughs often. Spread on a large table, an assortment of sunlit bottles with eye-catching labels stand beside oval trays arranged with vividly colored fruits, fresh breads, and various kinds of cheese. The girl searches for a hostess, but fortunately there is none. Judging by his efforts, she concludes, he's managed very well alone. Chatting with his friends, trim men with various degrees of graying hair, she feigns interest in unlikely topics; nouvelle cuisine in one corner, Wittgenstein in another. At times her pain seems so well hidden, even she forgets one smile from him could shatter her delicate armor. He guides several guests at a time through the newly furnished house. Beneath a thin coat of paint, she detects the pattern of faded wallpaper. Outside bare windows, gently swaying leaves, too green for autumn, enhance her illusion of a stage set. As he shows a couple up the stairs, she summons her courage and follows them. In the master bedroom he averts his eyes as she stares at the double bed she'd chosen.

By the front door, an elderly woman waits for him, a jacket in her hands. Obediently, the man kisses the older woman's upturned cheek. Mimicking the older woman's gesture, the girl turns her cheek toward him, almost as a challenge. He kisses her lightly. They exchange a few parting words. When the man returns to his guests, however, his gestures seem less certain, his manner less lively, his comments less convincing, his laughter seldom heard after the girl leaves.

In the Valley

The Peruvian guide has stopped the van at a small dusty mudbrick village in the river valley to buy freshly baked bread just for her. But the woman ignores his efforts to please her; she stares out the window at desolate foothills and overcast sky. After all, she tells herself, he is paid to be nice. The two other travelers in the van are more congenial than the woman whose stony silence conveys her reproach. It is not the guide's fault she was afraid to come alone. Why blame him for her fear? She regards the other travelers with distain; they are tourists, while she, a seasoned traveler who always roams alone, has suddenly lost her nerve.

The fast flowing slate-colored river looks cold and uninviting to her. She sits a distance away from the others while they inflate the raft, and don life jackets. The guide shook his head in disappointment when she refused to join them. Here on the river bank she feels safe. She imagines the others swept downstream, helpless, as the river toys with them. To her, the water looks like long oily hair curling round and under jagged boulders, weaving, sucking; the river is a temptress who snags trees in her watery tentacles, and gurgles with delight. The river rearranges her banks with her disorderly locks, and licks skins of stone. Spray that reminds her of soiled lace leaps high in the air. Whitecaps sparkle. The woman shudders. The stone she grasps feels cold and clammy. Her shoes feel wet with mud. The others wave before they pass quickly out of sight. The Peruvian has strong muscular arms from years of rafting. He knows the secret language of the river, her hidden currents. He tests his maleness on her slippery curves. Only the van driver stays behind, but the woman ignores him.

Towering peaks rise from the banks of the river. Their presence disturbs her but she feels drawn to those dark ragged ridges. She feels like a snake about to shed its skin: faces, gestures, fragments of conversation rise to the surface, and disintegrate in air. She raises her eyes toward stone terraces high above. So alien, so inscrutable those vertical walls seem, and yet the mountains allowed the Incas to climb their precipitous slopes. The mountains allow the embrace of clouds. The mountains allow landslides and earthquakes. The mountains allow changing shadows to define their folds. What would happen she wonders, if she allowed her fear and anger to slip away?

She would feel the pulse of the mountains like giant

drums beating in her ears. She would feel tangled eucalyptus roots straining through rock and soil to the raging
muddy river below. She would feel boulders break and
split and tumble down the cliffs, crashing at the bottom.
She would feel the surging river squeeze, then tear
through her flanks, widening the void within her. Whipped
by wind and rain and hail, she would become the haunted
spirit of the mountains, chiselled and carved into shape.
Dust would fill her mouth, and satisfy her hunger. Unlike
eucalyptus roots she would blow with the wind,
unanchored, yet the wings of birds would pass out of her
sight. Like a dislodged rock she would roll and tumble
without direction. Mist would hide her eyes. Sun would
scorch her skin. And her skin would toughen, harden,
sprout the bluish cacti that speckle the mountains. She
would turn brown and gray and grayish green. Her
presence would be indistinguishable. Eucalyptus would
take root on her darkened body, dry scrub and an
occasional orchid would grow. Her hair like slender
swaying branches would break in the wind. Humming-
birds would nest in her hair. Butterfly wings would graze
her eyelids.

Down below she would see the Peruvian navigate the
river, and she would see the driver, his cap in his hand,
but she would not recognize the woman seated on the
stones.

Invaders

The invaders have followed me home from the movie. I can see their shadows swaying through the windows. It is not the trees that sway outside tonight. If I fall asleep they will take control of our minds. I will save us all by staying up; then they can't carve their cross on the backs of our necks. If I stay awake Mother and Grandma will not act different tomorrow; they will not eat live frogs in a single gulp; they will not pour a bottle full of saccharine into their coffee cups; they will not be sucked inside a whirlpool of sand and swallowed by a spacecraft below; they will not return as strangers. If only Father could save us, but Father sleeps in his own apartment. I will let Father tell me a story as usual when he comes to say goodnight. When he leaves I will pretend to be asleep but I will make sure the invaders don't follow him and find his hiding place. I know he can't stay here with me; my bed is too small, and Mother and Grandma don't want him around. I will stand guard while lying in my bed, protect my grandma while she unpins her hair which falls halfway to the floor. I will protect my mother while she smears lotions on her face though she will look like a Halloween mask. I will listen to Mother and Grandma snore in the double bed Mother used to share with Father. I will keep my eyes glued to the windows, my mind vigilant, alert, for if I sleep, Mother and Grandma and Father will not be who they are when I wake up.

At the Cafe

Two women in their thirties, traveling the back road through a lonely stretch of arid land on their way to remote temple ruins, stop at a roadside cafe.

'I can't remember anything. Did I behave badly last night?' the woman asks her friend.

'No worse than other nights when you are drunk,' the friend replies.

'Well, I guess it's better that I don't remember then. I have nothing to regret if I can't remember.'

'If you worry about behaving badly, perhaps it would be better if you didn't drink,' the friend remarks, as she watches the woman gulp her wine.

'Then I'd never sleep,' the woman sighs. But adds, 'I'd rather be drunk and fall asleep than pace the floor all night like you!'

The friend sips her soda in silence. It's better not to talk at all, she decides. She looks around the dark dingy room where several old men with straw hats lie drunk or asleep, their heads resting upon stained formica tables. Outside, two donkeys hitched to a post wait patiently for the midday heat to end; sand whirls round their feet. In a corner, a language neither of the women understand is spoken by a wild-eyed man to no one. The friend shudders at the sight, and glances at the woman calmly drinking wine.

Island

*O*n vacation, the girl from the city, who is shy and fifteen, visits distant cousins on an island in the south. She arrives at dusk in a mailboat from the mainland that brings news once a week. The girl's hosts, a sour-faced man with bloodshot eyes, and a wife with a wooden smile, show the girl around in a jeep. The island is wilder than the girl expected. Forests draped with veils of Spanish moss frighten her. Wild boar dart across the path. Swamplands and bogs suddenly appear between palms. Racoons flit through thickets. On the private preserve, wild bulls threaten; their feet thrash damp ground in dark woods.

The couple, who are caretakers, live in the mansion the owners rarely use; they live in isolation. The sour-faced man talks about the guest who was thrown from a horse bitten by a rattlesnake. 'Lots of poisonous snakes here,' he tells the girl. In the evening her cousin wears gold lamé shoes, a long black dress and a strand of pearls. They sit down to a formal dinner at a long table in a candle-lit room, served by a maid. Wearing mud-caked boots and the sweat-soaked khaki shirt and pants he's worn all day, the man carries a bottle of bourbon which he empties without using a glass. He warns the girl about taking walks alone: 'It's dangerous here when you don't know the way.' In the main hall, animal skins cover the floor, and trophies from distant safaris adorn the walls: tiger heads, and those of antelope, wild boar, and deer loom larger than life to the girl.

When she walks the girl stays near the mansion, though the rambling house with its myriad rooms scares her too. Sometimes the man drives her, but by noon he is usually drunk. When he takes her with him in the jeep, he slams the door, and swerves down the road, ignoring any sign of life that lingers in his path.

One day the man, who the girl can tell was handsome once, drives to the beach at the other end of the island. 'This place is magic!' the girl shouts, excited, forgetting herself, forgetting her fear of the man who lies down on the sand with his bottle.

Twisted silver tree trunks, uprooted, rot on bleached white sand; their shapes suggest the movements of a violent dance suddenly suspended. Conches, cones, and iridescent fans seem magnified; countless shells lie waiting for her hands to scoop them up. In awe, she stares at perfect patterns carved by water in wet sand while unfamiliar birds swoop nearby. For the girl the island is transformed: on the journey back her eyes discern every trembling shade of green; she listens with wonder as leaves rustle with the sound of unseen creatures. A jolt disturbs her reverie. She glances at the man behind the wheel. Only people are dangerous, the girl decides, clutching the door while he recklessly drives.

The Gray Place

Three strangers and a guide drift slowly down the river in a rubber raft, headed toward Inca ruins. Their paddles across their laps, the travelers — a woman, a girl, and a man — gaze at the mountains surrounding the river. The guide sits with his legs up on the side of the raft, his face turned toward the sun. The woman has never seen the sun so bright, so piercing. She feels as though she has suddenly awakened, and the world has awakened with her. The hard blue light defines every cactus, every shrub, every tuft of Spanish Moss on nearby slopes. Snow-capped peaks rise in the distance. Doves and songbirds zig-zag in the sky. Tall reeds gently sway on the banks.

In the bright light, the woman thinks about the grayness of her home: she wonders why she lives in a world so gray. She pictures the gray sky, the gray faces, the streets filled with shadows.

The guide takes a deep breath, and with a satisfied smile, stretches out on the side of the raft. He points out a granite mountain streaked with violet ore.

'An Indian village lives in a cave at the base of that cliff,' he says. 'They've turned their backs on the twentieth century. Even the entrance is camouflaged with rock piles.'

The man and the girl seem unimpressed, but the woman strains her eyes to see the entrance hidden behind the barricade of stone. At home I live like those Indians, she muses: I hide in dark rooms, behind closed blinds. She wonders why she feels alive only when she's far away.

The guide opens a can of beer and raises it to his lips. He smiles as he feels the coolness in his throat. Lulled by the heat, and the motion of the river, the man and the girl doze while the woman gazes at shimmering stones. A breeze ripples the river. Water tingles on her skin. A dog barks. She waves to small children on the bank. Tall stalks of maize hide mud-brick huts with thatched roofs. On the steep mountainside, small green farms look like oasis on dry dusty slopes. Even parched cliffs, pockmarked with looted Inca tombs, glow reddish-gold. The guide steers the raft through a narrow channel between jagged rocks.

The dazzling sunlight fills the woman with hope: perhaps she could keep her sense of wonder, her feeling of aliveness if she stayed here. Why must gray be the indelible color of my life? she asks herself. She looks at the guide; his sinewy muscles, his golden skin, his hair flecked with silver. Like a little girl she sees a knight in shining armor; a man with the magic power to keep the grayness away.

'I don't want to go home, she says to the guide.

'You have two more weeks,' he says. 'Why think about it now?'

'Two more weeks aren't enough,' she replies.

'You can see a lot in two weeks,' the guide says.

'I don't care about seeing sights. I just want to feel alive like this every day.'

The guide smiles, their eyes meet, but he is silent.

'I want to feel content all the time. Do you think that's possible?' she asks him.

'No one is content all the time,' says the guide.

'If this was my home, I'd be content,' she says.

'When you travel, you see things with different eyes,' says the guide. 'You wouldn't feel the same way living here.'

'You seem content, and you live here,' the woman says.

His clear eyes stare into the distance. He decides to say nothing. Why spoil her dream? The man and the girl regard the woman with curiosity. But the woman is barely aware of their presence as she looks out at the river, the mountains, the sky.

Two Girls

*T*wo young girls, fresh from school, share an apartment near the river. The six-storey walk-up where they live, is old, run-down: they love it. Paint peels off the walls. The rent is cheap. They roll-up the rug and rearrange the meager furnishings left by the last tenant. In the evening when they return from part-time jobs, they listen to records and eat TV dinners. Both pretty, they easily meet boys they bring back to the two tiny rooms. The boys often stay overnight; one with the girl in the bedroom, the other with the girl on the foldaway couch in the front. First they smoke some dope and listen to music. Sometimes, on impulse, late at night, the girls roam dark streets to find an all-night deli and buy some sweets, or they sit in cafes till dawn where they meet actors, artists, writers.

At their graduation, their mothers met for the first time. Each mother insisted that her daughter was lazier, meaner, more selfish, more rebellious, more promiscu-

meaner, more selfish, more rebellious, more promiscu-
ous. The girls, one eighteen, one nineteen, pay no attention
to their mothers. Childhood sorrows are almost forgotten. But one of the girls secretly worries: maybe she
doesn't deserve this happiness, this freedom: later on,
there may be a price to pay.

Pretend

This is not the rainy season. But one day a storm floods the village. Water races wildly down the sloping streets. She loves the rain, this long thin girl with dreaming eyes. She is twenty-three and a foreigner. She stands barefoot on the cobblestoned street, knee-deep in water. She loves the rain because it is unexpected. It makes her forget. She doesn't have to pretend pleasure. This is pleasure, standing knee-deep in the rain.

She lies in the hammock slung across her roof. At one end stands a tiny whitewashed house that she reaches with a ladder. Below by the well women hang their dripping clothes to dry. No one will stop her here. No mother of hers will scream. No husband can bring her back now. Here she pretends all she wants. Each morning on her way to school she meets villagers who tip their straw hats. They know her now. They see her everyday. She says hello in their language. Not much else. She doesn't make much effort. Hello is enough.

The teacher speaks a language she understands though he is a foreigner from a country different than her own. He speaks her language and the language of the country fluently. He came here after the war, after he was shot. You can see him limping a mile away with his wooden leg. It's a mystery to her why he lives in this town, why he teaches sculpture at the school. They say he was a famous sculptor in his country. Here he lives hidden away behind high bushes surrounding his patio, his house. He's very private. No one knows him well.

She would like to know him well but she keeps distance. Even while she works she dreams. She makes it impossible for anyone to get close. Even when she watches she dreams.

There is nothing really interesting to see about him because he acts all the time as though he is being watched. Maybe that's because he was in a camp during the war, but she's sure he knows she's always watching. When he speaks to her she only acts as though she's miles away. She's embarassed then, she's afraid he knows her dreams. He doesn't speak to her often. He doesn't know why she comes to class. She's already a sculptor, already had shows in her country. She told him her husband comes from the country he left. He knows her husband is also a sculptor. He knows she came here to get a divorce but her husband isn't worth the expense, she said. Instead she's using the money to live here for awhile.

She wants the teacher to tell her what to do, like her father, her husband. Then she can get angry. Then she can rebel. Then she knows they are connected. The teacher is very careful with his words. He can tell she's a volcano, still now, but easy to erupt. He doesn't say her work is good or bad. He says she is a hard worker, really works. She doesn't need his advice, but she wants his advice anyway. He gives it only when she asks him more than once. He doesn't want to get involved. After all, he has a wife and children, a whole world she doesn't know about, like her father, who had a wife she didn't know about, until years after his death. She never knew there was a wife between the first one and her mother.

The model in class is very pretty, very shapely. She wishes she was as pretty though she is and doesn't know it. She wonders if the model is the teacher's lover. Nothing she has seen or heard has suggested this, but still she wonders. She keeps distance from the men in class because she's not sure where she stands. The men are foreigners like herself. When she talks to the men she tells them about her husband. She wonders why they keep their distance. She doesn't notice when they flirt, when they seem interested. She's afraid these men will be like her father who abandoned her, or like her husband. Her husband sends her letters and pretends that everything is alright between them. He opens her mail in her absence, and tells her what she's missed.

She rents the roof top room from the family who live below. Several families live in houses clustered round the well. The men are rarely home. Late at night she hears them come home drunk. Most of them work in a factory in a neighboring town. The women stay at home and look after children. She wonders if the children go to school. They pull at their mother's skirts and cry out. The women are good-natured. They laugh and talk all day long. They leave her alone. They forget that she lives here. That's just the way she wants it.

Before she lived in the roof top house she lived with a girl from a small town who had worked in an office. This girl was also a foreigner. They shared two rooms to save money. They made some trips together. She persuaded the girl from a small town to hitch-hike with her. The small town girl was scared. After the second trip the small town girl wouldn't go away with her anymore. Then she found the roof top room. She hadn't liked the girl much anyway. She just wanted company. She just wanted to know someone was there.

Inside the tiny roof top house is a bed and a chair and a wood shelf across two neat piles of bricks. On the wood shelf sits a worn clay water jug she bargained for in the market. It was the pedlar's water pot. New ones for sale didn't interest her. She only wanted the one that was used. The one that bore scars. She liked the dark spots on the surface. She liked the shape. It is awkward, handmade. In her house it is an ornament. She never uses it. She likes to look at it. She buys things that will remind her later on of the places she has seen. In her room she only wants to see what is beautiful. Practical items she keeps stuffed in her suitcase. She doesn't want to see anything that will remind her of chaos, disorder. Everything chaotic, disturbing, must be hidden away. If she doesn't see it she can pretend it doesn't exist. She pretends this way with people too: since her mother isn't here she has no mother, since her husband isn't here she has no husband. She has only her father. In the roof top room she can be alone with her father and no one will know.

She meets a blond-haired man she likes. She meets him at the school which is a former palace. He is not a student. He is passing through on his way to somewhere else. He has a wife at home but they don't get along. He drives her in his car to a town with a very large market. They spend all day browsing through the stalls. He buys her little presents. Late at night she takes him to her roof top room. He follows her up the ladder. They lie on the narrow bed

and stare at the ceiling. Something isn't right she feels.
He doesn't push her. When he leaves the next morning
she feels ill for several days. They send each other letters.
From another town, some months later, she will call him
on the phone. His wife will answer. The man will get
upset. Their friendship will be spoiled.

During the school break she travels south alone. The
dingy bus station and the poor dirty people frighten her.
In the bathroom urine floods the floor. She almost chokes
from the smell. In the crowded bus she squeezes in the
back seat between a family. She shares the blanket when
they go to sleep. For many hours the bus bounces down
dirt roads, all night and half the following day. Here she
doesn't have to think. She can't think.

In the seaside town she wanders down the only street
and rents a tiny room. She spends her days lying on the
beach, pretending she is somewhere else. Time goes
slowly while she waits for the moment when she will
know what to do. She watches giant tortoises flat on their
backs, slowly dying in the sun. She walks through the
forest and buys a trinket, a clay figure, from a pedlar she
meets on a path. She smiles at barefoot children who
follow her past their thatched roof huts and laugh. They
have never seen a foreign woman before.

Back in the little town she sits in the square every
afternoon and waits for a man who doesn't want her. He

was an engineer once before he came here. He is in her class. He is having an affair with a married woman who is older than he is. She sits in the square and waits for him to pass and say 'Hello'. They will talk a few minutes and then he will go away. Then she will pretend to read her book. She is saving his words for later. She will think about his words at night. When she is too tired to be angry at her husband, her father, she will lie down on the bed in the dark and think about his words. She will add a few words of her own to those he said. She will say them to herself in a different tone than the one he used to say them. She will add a look in his eyes that wasn't there. She will change his smile so that his smile is just for her. When she will see him tomorrow at school she will barely recognize his face.

Reincarnation

The English teacher in the eighth-grade class has asked each student to choose a topic and write a story. One girl has written a story called *Reincarnation*. The teacher, an elderly spinster, old fashioned, and easily irritated, wonders what a thirteen year old knows about reincarnation, wonders why a pupil would choose this topic. The teacher is also annoyed by her own ignorance of the subject. In the story, set in India, Brahma bulls wander freely through the courtyards of a palace. A girl is reborn as a princess, her reward for being a good girl in a past life. Her father is reborn as a prince. The prince and princess marry and live happily ever after. The teacher, shocked by the story, thinks about the girl who struck her as odd from the start. She remembers a note written by the girl's father to excuse her absence one day. The note, almost illegible, made the teacher wonder if the man was illiterate, or foreign. The girl never raises her hand in class; she often stares out the window while the teacher speaks: to the girl, this life is only a dream.

Paradise

In the sweltering midday heat, two American girls wait impatiently on line at the air strip for the small plane that will fly them inland to the jungle ruins. On one side of the runway stands a plane wreck, at the spot where it crashed years ago. The girls arrived at dawn, but when the old plane rattled down the runway, three hours late, a crowd of locals emerged from a shack, rushed on board, and left the tourists standing wide-eyed. Determined to catch the next plane, the girls wait outside behind a young frail-looking blonde, her arms loaded with bundles. To the girls, her skirt and blouse and low-heeled pumps seem terribly old-fashioned, her outfit odd for a jungle jaunt. The more impatient girl, small and green-eyed, raises her voice when the guard steers her back in line. The other girl, tall and dark-eyed, sighs and shakes her head. Turning to the girls, the blonde says, 'Impatience won't help. I know. I'm a missionary here.' The small girl stops stamping her foot, and looks in surprise at her angelic face.

The American missionary lives among a remote Indian tribe in an isolated village in the jungle. Once a year on her vacation, she visits the capital with a list of requests. This time she ordered forty toilets for her tribe. 'The Indians get worms from walking in their feces,' she says, while adjusting a hairpin in her untidy bun. The small girl who stiffens as a wasp circles her head, wonders how anyone could live here.

When they arrive in the town near the ruins, the missionary rents a boat by the lake, and invites them to visit her friends, an Indian couple who run a restaurant on a small lush island. The girls look for signs of the establishment from the dock, but only a crude wood table with two benches stands outside their mud-walled hut. Dogs, children, and chickens dart in and out of the bush. While the missionary converses with her friends in their native tongue, the girls swim in the cool calm water.

'Aren't you afraid of terrorists?' the small girl asks when the missionary joins them.

'No,' she replies. 'I am more afraid of the German airport which will be built in several years.'

The turquoise lake turns to saphire as the sun sets. Rose and amethyst hues streak the sky. Fragrant frangipani and papaya trees fade as the forest vibrates with the sound of night creatures. Fireflies outshine the lights on shore. 'This place is paradise!' the small girl says, floating serenely on her back. The tall girl, floating beside her, agrees. The girls have forgotten the landing strip, forgotten the stifling air. The missionary dries off on shore, says she will retire early; she still has a six-hour journey by jeep to her village.

In the water, the girls imagine the idyllic lives they could lead on the shores of this lake: the small girl can see herself sketching under palm and zapote trees, a frangipani blossom in her hair; the tall girl can see the vacation house she would build, the house boy who would cook her meals, the Latin lover who would share her bed. The girls glance in the direction of the missionary who carefully braids her long blonde hair.

Fun

The girl in the painting class renders the model on canvas with small precise brush strokes. The result is very effective. Only when the teacher says, 'Where is the background?' does the girl see that her painted figure stands in blank white space. She has no idea what to paint in that empty space. The painting looks right to her the way it is; there is nothing in the background, nothing to distract from the figure; the figure is alone in the space like the girl painting in the class of twelve.

'You should become a painter,' the teacher remarks in a flippant tone.

'It's not fun,' the girl replies.

'Fun! Why should painting be fun?' the teacher asks.

'I don't want to do anything that isn't fun,' the girl replies, with a face so sad one would think she never smiled.

Night Song

Pleased that the others in her group decided to remain in Lima, the woman looks forward to a private Amazon tour with the guide. Waiting for them at the air strip in the jungle, a tall American man towers over his Indian driver as they stand beside a battered car.

In late afternoon they drive down the muddy road between the tangle of trees and lianas, passing wooden shacks on stilts against the floods. Ignoring the woman, the guide and the tall man talk about mutual friends. The woman, too dazed to feel slighted, doesn't notice the guide's weary eyes. At the river, hugged by low dense jungle, the threesome board a launch to take them downstream to the tall man's lodge. The woman gazes at the water reflecting pink and gold and violet slashes in the sky. She listens to the echoing laughter of children, bathing beside the boat. The magic of the river seeps through her skin like a healing potion giving life. She feels peaceful despite the raucous shouts and loud music from the bars along the dock. Suddenly the world she knows feels so far away she wonders if it really exists. She wonders if she will ever want to leave despite the tall man's mention of piranhas, and the swarm of mosquitoes buzzing round her head.

At the lodge, beneath the enormous thatched dome of the main hall raised on stilts, pet toucans, parrots, and a pair of brilliantly colored macaws fly about the room. The tall man's wife strokes a spider monkey squirming on her lap while the woman wonders why the tall man evades her eyes. After dinner, the guide, exhausted by his three-week tour, retires early to his bungalow so the woman ventures out with the tall man's wife. In the clearing before the lodge, a dozen vultures pluck small fish from puddles left by the floods. Like giant tear drops, oropendola nests hang down from the branches of a tree. Stars shimmer through the leafy canopy of jungle near the river. On the muddy trail, the wife hacks through the brush with a machete. 'Everything is alive!' cries the woman, as the sounds of a million creatures vibrate in her ears. She's not alone. She is part of this night song which celebrates each passing day. She has forgotten her fears of deadly vipers, and her fantasies about the guide. The wife turns her flashlight toward the marsh, hoping to spot the eyes of a cayman, but instead the beam spotlights a tarantula on the side of a dug-out canoe. Amazed, the woman stoops to look at the creature whose body is larger than her hand.

In the dim light of the lodge, the tall man drinks a beer. Another bloody tourist with jungle fever, he thinks to himself. He closes his eyes, and tries to forget the torrential rains, the steaming air, the leaden skies day after day, the termites, the endless repairs, the lazy Indians who steal behind his back, who show no gratitude. In the glowing face of the woman — as she enters the room — he sees his dream before it cracked like a mirror, and splintered in a thousand shards. But the woman sees only the spider monkey swinging from the rafters, dancing to the night song still ringing in her ears while the guide tosses in his sleep.

The Fun House

*H*er plane delayed till mid-afternoon, the woman wanders through downtown Lima. To kill time, she enters the only museum open in early morning. She wanders through exhibits in damp cavernous halls, replicas of Spanish torture chambers after the conquest.

His limbs strapped down, a figure about to be pulled apart on a rack, stares wide-eyed. The feet of another are slowly burnt. One is forced to drink hot lead. Others, in a dungeon, squat in metal cages, four foot square. Locks, chains, whips, leg irons, bracelets studded with spikes adorn the walls.

The exhibits remind her of the Fun House at the amusement park back home. She vividly remembers riding with Father through the Chamber of Horrors. She recalls the ghoulish laughter, the devilish faces that leaped from trapped doors, then vanished in darkness.

Here, the badly painted wooden figures wearing pe-
riod costumes look like caricatures even in dim light. The
executioner's painted eyes seem as dead as his victim's.
The victims stare with open mouths and arms askance,
but they look more like singers than victims.

In the Fun House with Father, she would scream, but
she was never afraid: she was thrilled, excited. Even then
she knew how Father enjoyed her shrieks of delight. She
walks through the ramped passageways, smiling. As she
leans over the rail before the exhibit of a man burning at
a stake, she is still smiling. She doesn't see the Peruvian
family staring at her, wide-eyed.

Distraction

The guide only feels alive in the presence of danger. But here, on this quiet channel in the Amazon, there are no wild rapids to traverse, no whirlpools or eddies to skirt, no steep mountains to climb. Even piranhas don't disturb the bathing Indians. Cayman, electric eels, and sting rays pose no threat to passengers gliding down the river in a launch. The likelihood of a fer-de-lance or an anaconda sneaking on board is slight. Here, the guide seems tired; only the constant buzz of mosquitoes keeps him awake while the woman, enraptured, gazes at bromeliads, ferns, and orchids growing high on the trunks of towering trees. After intervals of silence, she besieges him with questions; she wants to know by name, all the plants and flowers, butterflies and birds within her field of vision. Her questions annoy him, but wishing to appear helpful, he turns to his guidebook. Reluctantly, his eyes follow the flight of birds but they disappear too fast. The jumble of trees and roots and vines look all the same to him. In answer to her questions, the guide picks names at random, and reads them out loud. But the woman forgets each name as her attention shifts with each new scene.

When the launch gets stuck in a dense tangle of water hyacinth covering a stretch of the channel like a thick field of flowers, the guide perks up. He watches intently as the boatman thrashes through the maze of roots with a machete, but he loses interest when the boat begins to move. Unlike the woman he can't stand being still and solitary; he doesn't like to think or meditate; he is a man of action. He feels trapped, hemmed-in by the cloud-filled sky, the monotonous jungle greenery enclosing him. The thatched hovels of Indian families dispersed along the river make him sad. He misses his two children who he rarely sees now that they live with their mother. He wishes he could visit them more often, but his work keeps him far away. He longs to find a woman to share his life, and envies a friend of his who is in love. He thinks about how weary he feels, how flabby he's grown, how strong he was at twenty-one. When a new stream of questions flow from the woman's lips, the guide welcomes the distraction, and eagerly turns a random page in the book.

Father

*H*er fther stands there. By now she is almost his age. Death hasn't changed his features, nor the gleam in his eye. She is still his little girl though her hair is turning gray. There is an awkward silence between them. She hadn't expected his visit. He wears a new and elegant suit. Did he walk into a shop and try it on? Did he scrutinize himself in a mirror? Does a mirror reflect a dead man? He settles in a chair, makes himself comfortable. 'I know I'm the cause of all your troubles,' he says, sadly. 'I'm here to see if I can help.' The daughter says, 'I've forgiven you long ago for leaving me.' As though he hasn't heard, he looks at his watch: 'I've only been allowed one hour,' he says. She throws her arms around his neck, and he hugs her the way he did when she was a child. They sit like that, in silent embrace, for almost an hour. Then he looks at his watch again. 'Perhaps it was wrong of me to come,' he says, with a sigh. 'No, no,' the daughter says, 'Now I can tell you, you gave me great happiness! That's why your leaving was so hard to bear. But now I know you never really left. This time will be easier.' He walks to the door, his head lowered. 'I wish I could do more,' he says. 'You've done all you can,' she tells him, her arm around his shoulder as he steps out into the corridor. 'Thanks for coming!' she calls out after him, as a neighbor looks down the empty hall.

Mist

The rain has stopped, but in mid-morning the sky is as dark as dusk. Dense mist hangs like a heavy curtain hiding great black peaks plunging two thousand feet to the river below. A narrow treacherous path of broken stones — a drunkard's vision of stairs — winds its way up a steep mountain slope. The Peruvian guide moves quickly. Occasionally he turns around, but he cannot see the woman. He pauses, wonders if he should wait, but remembers her coldness when he offered his help before.

Far behind she struggles over wet wobbling stones. She feels suspended between heaven and earth: she imagines the world below small as a globe on a school boy's desk. She hesitates before each step, and carefully plans her next foothold. Her hands search for something to grip, but the cold rock wall, smooth and slimy, provides no support. Tall grasses, ferns, and vines half-hidden by mist, break in her hand. Twigs snap underfoot.

Her eyes search nervously for the guide. Why has he run ahead? she wonders. Where is his hand to raise her from the mud? She knows, however, if she grabbed his hand she would hate herself for needing his help. If he was here, watching, she would feel like a helpless child. He doesn't care, she tells herself, though the day before she thought him a nuisance: why wouldn't he leave her alone on the rocks overlooking the river? Did he think she would fall into the turbulent water? Did he think she would throw herself against the jagged rocks? Perhaps he just felt friendly. Perhaps he didn't know he disturbed her solitude. Perhaps she felt angry because she recognized her loneliness in the moment when he joined her, and was afraid he'd read her mind.

Despite her fear she hoists herself up. With each step she feels a small thrill of victory. Even the mist so leaden a moment ago, seems luminous, as though a warm light had suddenly suffused the shroud of gray. She pauses. Cobwebs glitter with rain drops. She glimpses the curve of a bird's wing. Her hands touch leaves thick as lemon peels. Thin fingers of ferns brush her face. Spanish Moss gently sways in the wind. She sees the tangle of tall leafy plants entwined by vines. Yellow flowers grow in crevices above her head. Slowly she becomes aware of the bounty of life surrounding her; a paradise blooms with unnamed specimens.

At the top the Peruvian sits quietly waiting, his blue

eyes gaze at looming black peaks half-hidden by moving veils of mist. When she sees him a frown appears upon her face. 'Why didn't you warn me the climb would be so steep?' she says. The guide says, sighing, 'The gatekeeper walks here every day.' He points out a small thatched hut near the ruined Inca gate. A broad-faced Indian sits motionless inside. A few fallen boulders, the remains of an altar, leave the woman unimpressed. But the guide has brought her here to see the view. The mist and the mountains, however, seem unearthly, unreal to her. She feels slightly dizzy, her head aches: she imagines herself adrift on a pinnacle floating through an endless sea of mist. On impulse the guide removes his jacket, and does push-ups on the stony surface. His display of vanity surprises her, seems out of character; she imagined he was unaware of his good looks. As she watches his muscular arms, she not only desires him, she desires to be him: she envies his courage, his energy, his strength.

He stays close behind her as they descend. But this time the stones seem placed precisely for her steps. Her nimble feet surprise her. She feels propelled by an invisible engine. The mist has lifted. Her mind is clear. Feeling light as air, she dances over earth and stone, awakened, alive, in tune with the nature which seemed so forbidding, so remote. At the bottom of the slope when he knows she is safe, the guide resumes his normal pace, and leaves her far behind. But she is still giddy, dancing, gliding over the muddy terrain as she watches him disappear.

About the Author

The Daughter is Roberta Allen's second book. About her first, *The Traveling Woman*, *The New York Times Book Review* said, "...quicksilver dreams in which a single word or gesture is the exact metaphor for the separation between a man and a woman. Think of these stories as koans, or comments on the human condition...." Writing in the *Village Voice*, Gary Indiana called Allen's work "thoroughly enjoyable...full of lightning-like emotional illuminations. Her evocation of the feeling of foreign places and the erotic waywardness they inspire is exactly right."

A visual and conceptual artist as well as a writer, Allen's work is found in the permanent collections of the Metropolitan Museum of Art, the Museum of Modern Art, and the Cooper–Hewitt Museum in New York City, the Bibliothèque Nationale in Paris, and in many other museums in Europe, Australia, and throughout the United States.

SEMIOTEXT(E) USA

JIM FLEMING & PETER LAMBORN WILSON,
EDITORS
DESIGNED BY SUE ANN HARKEY

A huge compendium of works in American
psychotopography. Anarchists, unidentifed flying
leftists, neo-pagans, secessionists, the lunatic fringe
of survivalism, cults, foreign agents, mad bombers,
ban-the-bombers, nudists, monarchists, chidren's
liberationsists, zero-workers, tax resisters, mimeo
poets, vampires, xerox pirates, pataphysicians,
witches, unrepentant faggots, hardcore youth, poetic
terrorists… The best of current American *samizdat*.

LUSITANIA
KULTURA CONTROL

MARTIM AVILLEZ, EDITOR

A collection of essays on the theme of cultural
control — control by, of and through culture — as
conducted by multi-national corporations,
industrial capital, mass media conglomerates,
artistic elites, dominant cultural ideologies, and the
like. Profusely illustrated, and a bi-lingual edition,
with all material in Portuguese as well as English.

ON AN(ARCHY) AND SCHIZOANALYSIS
ROLANDO PEREZ

Using the "anti-oedipal" insights of Gilles Deleuze and Félix Guattari's classic work on capitalism and schizophrenia, Perez argues for "anti-fascist strategies in everyday life," and reads Nietzsche, literature, films and popular culture to critique deep political sympathies and antagonisms. Treats writers from Kafka to D. M. Thomas, filmmakers like David Lynch, punk music and feminist theory.
NOW AVAILABLE — $10 POSTPAID

SCANDAL
ESSAYS IN ISLAMIC HERESY
PETER LAMBORN WILSON

A search for the "poetic facts" of heresy in Islamic history, ranging from "sacred pederasty" in Persian sufism and forbidden imagery in Islamic art, to the inner teachings of the Assassins, the heretical influences on "Shiite terrorism," and the mystical uses of wine, opium and hashish, by the author of *Drunken Universe* and *Angels: An Illustrated Study*.
NOW AVAILABLE — $11 POSTPAID

THE ARCANE OF REPRODUCTION
HOUSEWORK, PROSTITUTION, LABOR & CAPITAL
LEOPOLDINA FORTUNATI

One of Italy's leading feminist writers and teachers critiques the traditional received Marxist categories for understanding the nature of capitalism and capitalist production and their effects on the "reproductive" role of women's labor and bodies.

FALL, 1992 — $12 POSTPAID

HORSEXE
ESSAY ON TRANSSEXUALITY
CATHERINE MILLOT

A study of transsexual desire, with chapters on the female drive in psychosis, SheMales, the sex of the angels, the Skoptzy sect of Eastern European transsexual *castrati,* sex-change operations, and much more, by a Lacanian psychoanalyst and professor at the University of Paris, VIII.
Illustrated.

(Cover art many bookstores won't display.)

NOW AVAILABLE — $12 POSTPAID

FILM & POLITICS
IN THE THIRD WORLD
JOHN DOWNING, EDITOR

The only anthology of its kind in English, with critical articles — most of them written by Third World writers — on leading figures and national cinemas, including analyses of important single films, political/aesthetic manifestoes, and interviews with directors from Africa, China, India, Turkey, Iran, the Arab World, the Philippines, Cuba, Latin America, and more.
NOW AVAILABLE — $12 POSTPAID

MARX BEYOND MARX
LESSONS ON THE GRÜNDRISSE
ANTONIO NEGRI

A key figure in the Italian "Autonomia" Movement reads Marx's *Gründrisse,* developing the critical and controversial theoretical apparatus that informs the "refusal of work" strategy and many other elements so crucial to this "heretical" tendency in Marxist theory. A provocative challenge to both capitalist and / or socialist apologists for waged slavery, whether by private business or the State.
NOW AVAILABLE — $12 POSTPAID

A DAY IN THE LIFE
TALES FROM THE LOWER EAST SIDE
ALAN MOORE & JOSH GOSCIAK, EDITORS

This provocative anthology of voices old and new
from New York's East Village will offend those
who like their literature quaint, pretty, and much too
tidy to touch. Stories reflecting the turbulent mosaic
of artists, ethnics, poets, junkies, barflies, radicals,
mystics, street people, con men, flower children,
losers, screwballs and professional eccentrics that
inhabit the city's edgiest neighborhood. Allen
Ginsberg, Ted Berrigan, Herbert Huncke, Lynne
Tillman, Ed Sanders, Miguel Piñero, Emily XYZ,
Zoe Anglesley, Jorge Cabalquinto, Cookie Mueller,
Ron Kolm, and many more, with art by Seth
Tobacman, Keiko Bonk, Martin Wong, and others.
An Evil Eye Book.
NOW AVAILABLE — $10 POSTPAID

AESTHETICS OF DISAPPEARANCE
PAUL VIRILIO

From infantile narcolepsy to the illusion of
movement in speed, the author of *Pure War*
and *Speed and Politics* and other works examines
the "aesthetic" of disappearance: in film,
in politics, in war, in the philosophy of
subjectivity, and elsewhere.
NOW AVAILABLE — $12 POSTPAID